This
Korky Paul
PICTURE BOOK
BELONGS TO:

Endpapers by Seung Jun Lee aged 9.
Thank you to SS Philip and James' Church of England Aided Primary School, Oxford
for helping with the endpapers.

For Sonna – R.T.
For Jesse Peter Mina, son and heir to a long line of moustaches – K.P.

OXFORD
UNIVERSITY PRESS

Great Clarendon Street, Oxford OX2 6DP

Oxford University Press is a department of the University of Oxford.
It furthers the University's objective of excellence in research, scholarship,
and education by publishing worldwide in

Oxford New York

Auckland Cape Town Dar es Salaam Hong Kong Karachi
Kuala Lumpur Madrid Melbourne Mexico City Nairobi
New Delhi Shanghai Taipei Toronto

With offices in

Argentina Austria Brazil Chile Czech Republic France Greece
Guatemala Hungary Italy Japan Poland Portugal Singapore
South Korea Switzerland Thailand Turkey Ukraine Vietnam

Oxford is a registered trade mark of Oxford University Press
in the UK and in certain other countries

British Library Cataloguing in Publication Data
Data available

ISBN: 978-0-19-272712-1 (paperback)

Printed in China

Paper used in the production of this book is a natural,
recyclable product made from wood grown in sustainable forests.
The manufacturing process conforms to the environmental
regulations of the country of origin.

www.korkypaul.com

Professor Puffendorf's Secret Potions

Written by Robin Tzannes

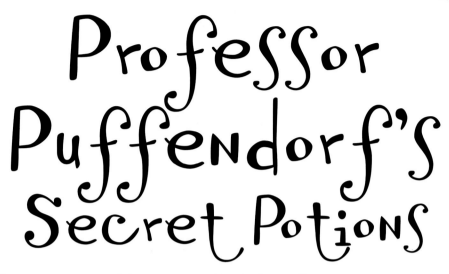

OXFORD

UNIVERSITY PRESS

Professor Puffendorf was the world's
greatest scientist.
You may have some of her inventions
in your own home: perhaps
Unburnable Toast, or a Banana-Matic,
or maybe a Smell-o-Telephone.

Professor Puffendorf's laboratory was a
wonderful place, full of odd-shaped
bottles and tubes, and strange-looking
machines that hissed and steamed and
spluttered and squeaked.

On a cluttered counter in this laboratory was a cosy cage, and in this cage lived a guinea-pig named Chip.

He was a friendly little creature, bright and clever.

Professor Puffendorf loved Chip,
and Chip loved her.

Professor Puffendorf's assistant
was a man named Enzo—a lazy,
grumbling fellow.

As he swept the floor he mumbled, 'Look at the professor, just sitting at her desk, while *I* do all the work! She's rich and famous, but whoever heard of poor, honest Enzo?'

And he swept the dust into a crack under the linoleum.

One day, when Professor Puffendorf was going to a conference, she said to Enzo, 'Please wash all the thistle tubes and dust the magdeburg hemispheres. And this time, *try* to remember to turn off the titanium blender when you leave.'

Then she put on her hat and went out.

As soon as the professor had gone, Enzo jumped into her chair and put his feet up on the desk.
'Ah, yes, *this* is where I belong!' he said, and helped himself to the professor's dish of peppermints.

Suddenly, his eye fell
on a cabinet marked
'TOP SECRET!'
This cabinet was locked
with two padlocks and
three combination locks,
and Enzo had been
told never, never
to open it.

But he forgot that now, and
rummaged through the professor's
desk until he found the keys and
combinations.

Soon the **'TOP SECRET'** cabinet stood wide open, revealing a colourful row of bottles filled with mysterious potions.

Enzo picked one up.
It said, **'HAIR TODAY**.
For thick, red, curly hair
instantly: take ten drops and
count to five.'

Enzo was about to put the bottle to his lips . . . but he hesitated.
He knew that many of the professor's **'TOP SECRET'** formulas had not been tested.

They might not work. They might even be poisonous.

Then Enzo had a wicked idea . . .

try it on the guinea-pig first!

He measured ten drops into Chip's
water bottle.
'Oh, Chippy,' he called, 'teatime!'

And as Chip drank the potion, Enzo counted anxiously . . .

1, 2, 3, 4. . .5!

It worked!
Chip's furry little head was
suddenly covered with thick,
red, curly hair.

Enzo began to prance around the laboratory, clapping his hands and singing, 'I'll be rich! I'll be rich! At last I'll be rich!'
He knew that many people would pay a great deal of money for **'HAIR TODAY'**.

So Enzo decided to steal the formula from Professor Puffendorf.

Enzo went back to the **'TOP SECRET'**
cabinet, to see what else he could steal.
The next bottle said, **'SWEET SONG.**
For a beautiful voice: six drops and
count to five.'

Enzo brought the bottle to Chip's cage and gave him six drops.

Then he counted . . .

1, 2, 3, 4, 5...

It worked.

Chip began to sing with a voice so rich and melodious that the tears came into Enzo's eyes.

Enzo could hardly believe his luck.

Why, that cabinet must be *filled* with rare and wonderful inventions, secret potions that would make him rich for the rest of his life.

'Now,' thought Enzo, 'I'll finally get what I deserve.'

He went to try a third bottle.
This one said, **'BEST WISH**.
One drop and count to five.
Your heart's fondest wish will
come true.'
Enzo's greedy eyes nearly
popped out of his head.

I'll wish to
be the boss! . . .

'BEST WISH! Why, this is all
I need. I'll just wish to be rich,
and famous, and . . . I know! . . .

No, the mayor! . . .

No, no, no! I'll wish to be the KING!'

But just as he was about to swallow the potion, he remembered . . . it might not have been tested.

Better give some to Chip first.

Enzo looked at Chip with an
evil glint in his eye.
With trembling fingers he
measured out one drop, saying,
'Make a wish, boy. Whatever
your little rodent heart desires.
A ton of alfalfa? A new
treadmill? You name it,
Chippy, and it's yours.'

Chip swallowed the potion obediently as Enzo counted . . .

IT WORKED!

When Professor Puffendorf came
back that evening she knew at once
what had happened.
The **'TOP SECRET'** cabinet
was open.
Chip was singing a magnificent
tune as he swept the floor.
And Enzo was running on the
treadmill.

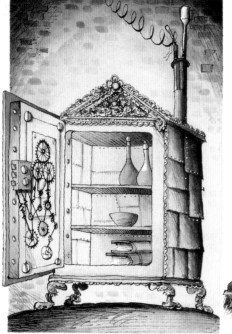

'You're a very silly man,' sighed the professor, shaking her head at Enzo. 'And you got just what you deserved!' She passed a sunflower seed through the bars of his cage.
'But don't worry, my dear. I'm sure I can get you out of this mess.'

'But first,' she continued, turning to Chip, 'I'm famished. Would you care to join me for tea and Unburnable Toast? And then perhaps a game of draughts?'
'Yes, thank you,' said Chip. 'That would be lovely.'

Then he put away his broom, hung up his coat
and followed the professor out of the lab . . .
remembering to shut off the titanium blender
as he left.

KORKY!

www.korkypaul.com